to Be a Pirate

By Sue Fliess

Illustrated by Nikki Dyson

A GOLDEN BOOK · NEW YORK

Text copyright © 2014 by Sue Fliess
Illustrations copyright © 2014 by Nikki Dyson
All rights reserved.
Published in the United States by Golden Books, an imprint of Random House Children's Books,
a division of Random House, Inc., 1745 Broadway, New York, NY 10019.
Golden Books, A Golden Book, A Little Golden Book, the G colophon, and the distinctive gold spine
are registered trademarks of Random House, Inc.
randomhouse.com/kids
Educators and librarians, for a variety of teaching tools, visit us at RHTeachersLibrarians.com
Library of Congress Control Number: 2012941289
ISBN 978-0-449-81309-6
Printed in the United States of America
10 9 8 7 6 5 4 3 2 1

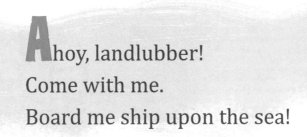

Ahoy, landlubber!
Come with me.
Board me ship upon the sea!

Not a pirate?
Don't know how?
Ye can learn to be one now!
Come in closer—
I don't bite.
A pirate ye shall be tonight!

First, I'll take ye
round the ship.
Deck is wet, so don't ye slip!

That's the mast.
There's the aft.
If she sinks, right here's the raft.

BURP!

Skulls and crossbones
mark our flags.
Never mess with
scallywags.

No more manners!
No more fuss!
When you're here, ye act like us.

Shuffle, swagger,
that's our walk.
Learn the lingo, talk the talk.

Gangway! Blimey!
Yo-ho-ho!
Those are words you'll need to know.

Wear an eye patch.
Hold a hook.
Ye can choose your pirate look.
Pick a parrot for your arm—
every pirate's lucky charm.

Rules for pirates?
Let's just say . . .
ye can throw *all* rules away!

No more toothpaste!
Farewell, bath!
once ye choose the pirate path.

I smell trouble
closing in.
Gives me shivers on me skin.
"Check the spyglass!
Enemy ship!"
Aim the cannons—let 'em rip!

The chase has started!
Never fear.
This ship's fast, and land is near.

Watch out, mateys!
Duck below!
Pirates heave and pirates ho.

We've outrun them,
missed their trap.
Make for shore and check the map.

Dock the vessel.

Knot the rig.

Grab your shovel—time to dig!

Find your treasure.
Don't be late—
soon you'll hold your piece of eight!

Sing a shanty,
whistle, dance.
Do a jig in pirate pants.

The test is over,
buccaneer.
You're a pirate now—
let's cheer!

17